THE RAINBOW ORCHID
VOLUME ONE

RYE JUNIOR HIGH SCHOOL
501 WASHINGTON ROAD
RYE, NH 03870

THE RAINBOW ORCHID
VOLUME ONE

GAREN EWING

EGMONT

BAÑANES GROPE
Guayaquil - Cherbourg - Portsmouth
via the Panama Canal

Port De Cherbourg
Entrepôt 8
Cherbourg, France

Monsieur Flue
under the direction of
Mr Urkaz Grope

EGMONT
We bring stories to life

First published 2009 by Egmont UK Limited, 239 Kensington High Street, London W8 6SA

Copyright © Garen Ewing 2009

The author has asserted his moral rights.

ISBN 978 1 4052 4853 2

1 3 5 7 9 10 8 6 4 2

Printed in Singapore

Charlotte – housekeeper

Sir Alfred Catesby-Grey – historical researcher

Julius Chancer – historical-research assistant

Lily Lawrence – silent-film actress

Nathaniel Crumpole – movie publicity agent

James Palfrey – musicologist

Nellie – housemaid

Lord Reginald Lawrence – aristocrat

Charles – chauffeur

Box – pugilist and henchman

William Pickle – Daily News columnist

Newton – botanist

Urkaz Grope – businessman

Evelyn Crow – personal assistant to Urkaz Grope

Scobie – butler

George Scrubbs – Daily News photographer

Pendleby – to be revealed

Winston Attle – to be revealed

Mr Drubbin – field agent

Ansel – mechanic

Eloise Tayaut – aerobat

Benoît Tayaut – barnstormer

Josette Tayaut – aerobat

CHK!
CHK!
CHK!

Sir Alfred Catesby-Grey
Ancient & Historical
Research

J. Chancer Asst.

DRRIIIIINGG!

Good morning, I'm here to
see Sir Alfred. My name is
James Palfrey.

Quite a place
he has here!

This way, please.

Sir Alfred bought it from the
actor, Henry Irving, thirty years
ago, sir. This is the library.

Sir Alfred's private collection.

Fascinating...

What delightful orchids!

TOK
TOK

Enter!

Mr Palfrey! Nice
to see you again.

You have the manuscript, Sir Alfred?

I believe so.

This is my assistant, Julius Chancer. I must admit he did most of the work to find it.

Quite a task you set us, Mr Palfrey!

Oh my goodness!

I knew it existed! Polyphonic, as I thought...you can hear the beautiful harmonies just by looking at it!

I believe it is quite genuine, gentlemen...the manuscript to a lost opera by Henry Purcell!

Naturally, Mr Palfrey. We wouldn't have called you otherwise.

Here is the remaining payment. And I can't thank you enough. I'm deeply grateful, Sir Alfred.

A pleasure.

Just listen to it!

That's that then!

Eight months of clambering around dusty old attics, dismantling antique violins, searching for clues in Restoration poetry...and not to mention getting shot at ...twice!

I do believe you enjoyed every minute of it, Jules!

But we're only just keeping our heads above water, and there's nothing else on the horizon. You really should think about selling some of the artefacts.

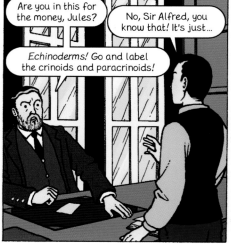

Are you in this for the money, Jules?

No, Sir Alfred, you know that! It's just...

Echinoderms! Go and label the crinoids and paracrinoids!

I get the message!

And don't forget the *Halkieria*. I want them all dusted!

Elsewhere...

Oi! You Pickle, the reporter?

That's me...

Got someone here, wants a word.

Woah! You'll have to make an appointment!

Who are you?

I work for Mr Urkaz Grope, and he's not a happy man, Mr Pickle.

I'm sure Charles Darwin here could bring a smile to his face...

I *really* would advise against insulting Box.

Now to get to the point. Mr Grope requests that you refrain from publishing anything concerning his botanical exploits.

I don't know what you mean.

Let me put it another way. How would you like to try writing with a broken arm?

Heh, well, I prefer to use a pencil, but...heh, heh!

I think you understand, Mr Pickle. Box, dispose of this Grub Street hack for me, will you?

Wait! I'm famous! You can't...

Think about it, reporter!

Yaaah!!

Pickle! Er... what are you doing down there?

Interviewing the pavement! What do you think?

Oh. Right. Well, come on, her train's just pulled in. I don't want to miss any good pictures.

There she is!

Lily! Are you here to make a new film?

Is it true Von Stroheim has signed you up?

Any truth to the rumours of romance with Douglas Fairbanks?

Will you return to the stage, Lily?

Will your father finance your next picture?

Have you fallen out with Fay Wray?

Any new Hollywood crazes?

Lily's back for a well-earned vacation after making six pictures this year!

Gentlemen, this is my American publicist from United Players, Mr Nathaniel Crumpole.

Miss Lawrence, you'll be opening the Wembley Botanical Exhibition while you're here?

It's an honour to be asked. This is its fifth year. Rudyard Kipling opened the Exhibition last year.

But this year it's Lily Lawrence!

And it's true, is it not, that your father will be entering the orchid competition once more?

Er, yes. That's true. He was last year's winner, in fact.

Of course, this year he has no hope of winning at all. Any comment?

Hold it with the applesauce, mister! I don't like your line. Stick to the movies!

Fine. Fine.

Lily, is it true that your father's wealth was your ticket in to Hollywood?

I WON'T HAVE IT!

Gimme that, you sap!

Sir...

...I deny you your power!

SNAP!

Hmmm...

Tell me more about sap, Mr Crumpole.

HA! HA! HA! HA! HA!

Charles is here with the Lincoln. Time we were going, Nathaniel!

Future interviews with Miss Lawrence by private appointment only!

Later, at the Whistling Duck...

So Pickle, what's all this about orchids? What are you up to this time?

My dear chap, you shall have to read tomorrow's *Daily News* to find out, just like everyone else!

Lily Lawrence Returns to England

Our reporter – William Pickle

Former bit-part player of the London Theatre, and now England's own star in the Hollywood sky, Lily Lawrence yesterday returned from the Californian lemon groves to the green parks of her ancestral home, Pitscally House, run by Daddy – Sir Reginald Lawrence, Earl of Baggall and owner of the large patch of Sussex land that title brings.

The latest thing in Hollywood is the 'Studio Agent'. Lily, currently signed to United Players, is stuck with a Mr. Crumpole, who uses brisk American language such as 'Applesauce' and 'Sap' to convey himself. The U.P. Press Release gave up more – Lily has most recently played Josephine to John Gilbert's Napoleon, and Little May in a film of the same name (yet to show on our own shores). Her next moving picture is with Edna Purviance, Chaplin's leading lady.

As for Sir Reginald, he hopes for a family celebration at the fifth British Empire Exhibition at Wembley Park in Middlesex, as he again enters the world famous orchid competition, to be opened by his very own 'Little May'. He may have won it last year with the flushing blooms of his Odontoglossum Nevadense, but alas, this year he will

Lily as 'LITTLE MAY'

be attending in vain. Yes, faithful readers, you read it here first – the orchid competition is a foregone conclusion, and all thanks to the entry of the practically unique black [pearl or]chid, to be put forward by 'b[usinessman] Mr Urkaz Grope.

So what is next for Lily[? Her] father may not take the priz[e, but] but he won't lack for the ex[...] will send his famous offsprin[g to] Hollywood in a few weeks with [...] where she can indulge in more [...] screen capers for the masses.

"...the orchid competition is a foregone conclusion, and all thanks to the entry of the practically unique black pearl orchid to be put forward by businessman, Urkaz Grope."

I wouldn't be surprised if this so-called reporter gets his stories out of thin air. A black orchid indeed!

It makes me think of the one flower that would shut them all up for good. You remember, Jules?

A flower that would create a bigger spectacle than a black orchid?

Come now, Jules. The Notebook of Theophrastus?

Of course. The rainbow orchid, sent to the Lyceum by Alexander. But over two thousand years ago!

True Jules, true. Yet while you were fighting for King and Country in the Dardanelles, I met a missionary in Lahore who had *actually* seen it.

Well, it's an interesting story...

Sir, there's a gentleman from the News Agency to see you. He won't say what it's about.

Then I won't see him, Charlotte.

Sir Alfred! Thanks for seeing me!

Oh!

Just a couple of very quick questions!

Very well. That will be all, Charlotte, thank you.

Great! William Pickle, *Daily News.*

So you're Pickle? Be brief!

To the point – just my style! Now, I heard you've dug up a lost opera by Henry Purcell. What can you tell me about it?

Nothing. Did Mr Palfrey send you here?

Not exactly, but...

Then I bid you farewell, Mr Pickle.

Sir Alfred, if you can just confirm...

There is the door. Goodbye.

Hey, aren't these orchids? Yes, I remember reading you were something of an enthusiast...

So, you'll be entering the Wembley Exhibition?

According to your story here, there's no point in anyone entering. Now, good day, Mr Pickle!

Second Place is very admirable, Sir Alfred. You could always enter anonymously to avoid embarrassment.

Perhaps get your butler here to show it on your behalf. Worth it for the prize money. By the way, how is business?

Butler!?

First, Mr Pickle, we're doing very well thank you. Secondly, if we wanted, we could enter a flower that would make your black orchid look like a dried-up old dandelion!

Jules!

I don't believe you. I've been assured there is nothing so rare as a black orchid.

A black orchid might be rare, but the rainbow orchid is spectacular! Urkaz Grope wouldn't stand a chance.

Julius! That is quite enough! Mr Pickle, you will leave now. There is no story for you here.

Well, you can't say I didn't try. Edith Sitwell is performing some of her poetry through a megaphone at the Aeolian Hall, so I'd better dash anyway.

Thanks for your time, Sir Alfred. Cheerio!

I just wanted to rock his boat a little. Meddling quidnunc!

Well, I hope our names don't end up in one of his gossip columns!

My job is just too easy sometimes!

The next morning...

...and this is my father, Lord Reginald Lawrence.

Father?

Um, yes...I was hoping you could evaluate a family heirloom. I think you'll find it of interest.

It's not the sort of thing I usually do, Lord Lawrence, but certainly, let's have a look at it.

Judging by the scabbard, I'd say a ceremonial blade...

...seventeen hundreds, perhaps 1750 or so?

Ah, no! The sword itself is much older. Lobated pommel, the quillons and these markings suggest...twelfth century!

Amazingly preserved, but the scabbard is much later. I wouldn't put a price on your sword, Lord Lawrence, it's probably priceless.

More than that, Sir Alfred. This sword is my history...

...and my future.

It was originally owned by the Lords of Stone. The great Tybalt Stone carried it in the Crusades where it was said the blade shivered violently in combat. It became known as the *Trembling Sword of Tybalt Stone.*

The last ever Stone, Lord Hugo, bequeathed the sword to Carminus Lawrence in 1445. He became the first Earl of Baggall, and inheritor of the Stone estate.

It has been guarded by my family for over five centuries. My father carried it during the march to Kandahar in 1880.

It's an amazing object Lord Lawrence, but you can't mean to sell it?

Mr Chancer, selling this sword would ruin me...and I have done something far worse...

...An acquaintance visited for dinner a few weeks ago. We also indulged in a couple of card games, nothing serious...

Another game of Le Truc, my friend?

Thank you, Reginald, but after losing twelve games, not to mention the entire contents of my wallet, I'll have to say no! More of my home-made!

He said he was going to enter the Wembley orchid competition. As he was a beginner, I encouraged him...

But you know nothing about horti:hic:culture! It would be a washte of your time! Now, letsh have another game of Tre Luc!

I've a better idea. How about a little bet?

A bet? Oh goody, exschellent idea! What about?

I say I will beat you in the orchid competition this year.

What!? Ha ha haaa ha! You? Esh:hic:cellent! How mush shall we bet?

No, not money. How about, oh, say that sword? If you win, I'll get you membership at the Embassy Club.

Now I'm not a gambling man, Sir Alfred, but you know when you're on a winning streak, and my guest was in a persuasive mood. Well, for some reason, I eventually agreed...

Whatever, old chap. You can't win :hic!: Now, pour me some more of your delicious home-made stuff!

You not having any?

And now you've learnt about his black orchid. This friend of yours is Urkaz Grope, I take it?

Sir Alfred, whoever holds this sword has claim to the lands of Stone and the title of Earl.

Five centuries of trust and honour will be lost!

Not to mention your wealth and fortune!

That's not fair, Sir Alfred. Money is nothing to the ancient oath made by my family to safeguard the Stone legacy!

Why don't you call off the bet, or just refuse to recognise it?

And break the knightly code that binds my heritage? I have already brought enough dishonour to my ancestors! Anyway... Grope refuses to listen.

Lord Lawrence, as much as I would like to, I don't see how we can help you in this situation.

It's very simple, Sir Alfred. I would like to buy, and I can't stress enough that money is no object, your rainbow orchid.

How on earth did you hear about the rainbow orchid!?

Uh-oh.

Your interview with William Pickle in this morning's *Daily News*.

I can't believe it! He actually printed... He says I'm going to enter the...Antique dealer! He calls me an antique dealer!

I'm sorry, Lord Lawrence, Pickle is an opportunist hack with a wild imagination. I have no such thing as a rainbow orchid. You've been had.

You...you mean you won't sell it?

I mean we don't have it. The flower's a myth...a legend!

Then it's all lost! Gone! Five centuries... oh...the end!

Wait! Pickle can't just have made it up!

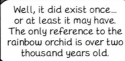

Well, it did exist once... or at least it may have. The only reference to the rainbow orchid is over two thousand years old.

Nnnnggg...!

Hojee!

POP!

That's almost as old as this valuable Phoenician pottery!

Sir Alfred, what are the chances...I mean, that missionary you mentioned in Lahore?

Not to mention the enormous cost of an expedition.

No Julius, it would be an impossible task. The chances of actually finding it would be tiny.

Sir Alfred, I *implore* you — if there's even the smallest hope of finding that flower...Cost is not a problem, name your price!

You *have* to find me the rainbow orchid!

Five minutes later, in the library...

Theophrastus was the successor to Aristotle and ran the lyceum for over thirty years. Only two of his works are thought to have survived.

Ah, thank you, Charlotte.

But two hundred years ago this was smuggled out of the secret archives of the Vatican. It was probably collected by Pope Nicholas the Fifth.

It is the fabled lost notebook of Theophrastus. And by the way, what you see here must not be mentioned outside of this room.

Er...would that include the Ideas Department at United Players?

Yes, even there, Mr Crumpole.

I don't wish to seem impatient, Sir Alfred, but what has all this to do with the rainbow orchid?

Most of his text is rather dry, a lot of theorising about roots, petals and seeds. But here...

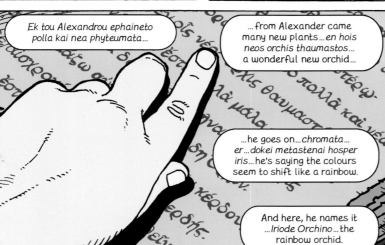

Ek tou Alexandrou ephaineto polla kai nea phyteumata...

...from Alexander came many new plants...en hois neos orchis thaumastos... a wonderful new orchid...

...he goes on...chromata... er...dokei metastenai hosper iris...he's saying the colours seem to shift like a rainbow.

And here, he names it ...Iriode Orchino...the rainbow orchid.

For any botanist the prospect of what Theophrastus describes is an exciting possibility. But here I have something that may add to its importance...

This is a copy of a stone tablet recovered from a ruined jungle temple in the Indus Valley.

I have not been able to translate the script, it is unknown, but here we can see, quite clearly, three orchids.

These orchids appear to sprout from rays fired by this figure here, who I'm certain is meant to be a form of the god Indra. Indra's bow was the rainbow.

It is just my own theory, but I believe this tablet gives us a contemporary glimpse of the rainbow orchid, tied in with some lost Vedic myth.

I don't quite understand. Are you saying the rainbow orchid grows in both Greece and India?

No, Lord Lawrence. Theophrastus received the orchid from Alexander on campaign in the Hindu Kush. Everything points to the flower growing in the northern subcontinent.

Very interesting, but none of this is particularly compelling evidence, is it?

It's certainly not conclusive, Miss Lawrence.

Sir Alfred...that missionary you said you met in Lahore?

Yes, well, I would be doubtful of the flower's survival into modern times were it not for Father Joseph Pinkleton.

Pinkleton worked among the Kalash. What's interesting about this tribe is that some believe them to be the descendants of Alexander the Great's soldiers.

He told me that one day a stranger came to the village selling remedies and tinctures. With him he had an orchid, the most amazing he'd ever seen.

He said it danced with light, shifting with colour, almost the exact phrase Theophrastus had written in his notebook so long ago.

The traveller wouldn't part with it, saying it was his protection. He also refused to reveal where the flower grew.

Tell me, Sir Alfred, do you believe the rainbow orchid exists?

I admit, Lord Lawrence, I do. But I also say finding it will be all but impossible. I do not believe an expedition is at all worthwhile.

Sir Alfred...

Julius! The dangers would far outweigh the tiny possibility of a reward. It would be like trying to find a needle in a field of haystacks! Populated by tigers!

Hmph! Black pearl orchid indeed! Before you even discuss the feasibility of an expedition, I'd see about this flower Urkaz Grope claims to own. Let's see if that exists!

Well...it should be easy enough to find out!

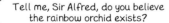

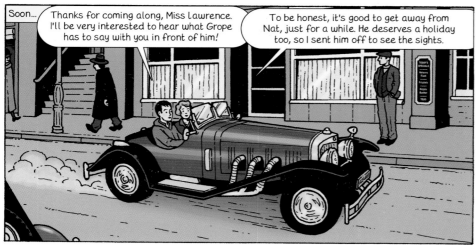

Soon... Thanks for coming along, Miss Lawrence. I'll be very interested to hear what Grope has to say with you in front of him!

To be honest, it's good to get away from Nat, just for a while. He deserves a holiday too, so I sent him off to see the sights.

Uh, Miss Lawrence...

Oh, just Lily, please!

Sorry, Lily. I can't understand why your father agreed to such a crazy bet. He stands to lose everything!

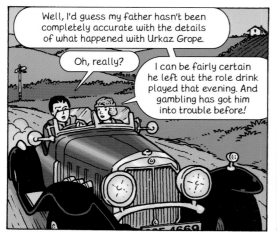

Well, I'd guess my father hasn't been completely accurate with the details of what happened with Urkaz Grope.

Oh, really?

I can be fairly certain he left out the role drink played that evening. And gambling has got him into trouble before!

Also, Grope can be quite intimidating. He has some kind of influence over my father, but I don't know why. They haven't known each other long.

I've never heard of Urkaz Grope. What does he do?

I'm not sure. All I know is he's extremely rich, but I have no idea what business he's in.

Well, perhaps we'll find out. Here we are!

CLONG!

Can I be of assistance?

We'd like to speak with Mr Urkaz Grope, please.

Please step inside, sir.

Hello!

And miss.

If you will remain here, I shall enquire after the master of the house.

Hello there.

Who? Me? Hello me?

You wouldn't be Mr Grope, would you?

Me? Oh no, ha ha... No. I wouldn't be him. I'm...

Newton! You shouldn't be out here!

Oh, I'm not! That is... er, I'm just leaving.

Off you go then. No hanging around.

Quite. Well, off I go then.

I'm Evelyn Crow, Mr Grope's personal assistant. He's very busy right now, can I help you at all?

Oh! It's Lily Lawrence, isn't it? I thought I recognised you.

Yes. Lord Lawrence's daughter.

Not to mention a movie star! Just imagine, a movie star in our very own hallway! How exciting!

Then you can probably guess why we're here. Mr Grope has made a bet with Lord Lawrence concerning the Wembley competition.

A bet? Well, a binding gentleman's agreement was reached between them, yes.

I understand you have in your possession a black pearl orchid. Can you prove you have such a flower?

You've been reading the newspapers. You can't trust the newspapers.

Scobie, will you show Miss Lawrence and her friend out, please?

Surely we have a right to know what we're up against?

Oh, it's just a silly little flower competition. Good luck!

Hmmm... clever, I suppose.

What do you mean?

It doesn't actually matter whether they have a black orchid or not. We still have to be certain of winning, whatever we face.

You know, I think I'd like a chat with our reporter friend, William Pickle.

Back in town...

You'd better wait here, Lily. We don't want to give Pickle more material for his column.

Hmm... good point!

Mr Pickle, there's a gentleman to see you.

Bring him in, Audrey, bring him in!

Ah, it's Sir Alfred's man... er, Jacob was it? Got more on that fabulous orchid of yours?

Julius Chancer, assistant to Sir Alfred Catesby-Grey.

Right! This is George Scrubbs, my photographer.

As we so generously provided a story for you yesterday, I wondered if you might care to return the favour. Just a couple of questions.

Fire away, my friend!

Have you seen Grope's black orchid?

Er... actually seen it?

No. We haven't even been able to meet Mr Grope himself yet!

You may not have met him, George, but I have!

What? When?!

Well... it doesn't matter! You weren't there!

No, I haven't seen his orchid, but he's got it. He's serious about winning the competition.

So... are you going to enter this rainbow orchid? When can I see it?

I might be able to persuade Sir Alfred. Do you know a man called Newton? Wide black hat, oversized doctor's bag?

Oh yes, Newton, he ...

No!

We don't know a Newton. Never heard of him. Who is he?

But William...

OW!

George, of course we don't know a Newton! You're thinking of, um, Newt...ting...ton ...Newtington! Tall chap, no hat. We just did a story on him. You're getting mixed up.

Newtington?

I see. Well... not to worry. I'll be in touch about the orchid.

Great! See you then.

Yes. Thanks for your help. Goodbye.

You prize idiot! Come on, I think it's time we paid Newton another little visit.

Newton.

McLEAN & PHIL

What's going on here?!

What films have you been in? Hey! Aren't you Rex Ingram?

Er, I'm not, no. Lily, we must get going now.

It's for my Auntie Millie. She loved you in *Foolish Women!*

Oooh! Take my picture too! Will I be famous?

Eh?

CLICK!

You know, George, sometimes these stories just seem to write themselves!

Why me?

The next day...

The Daily New

LAWRENCE ESTATE CONNECTED WITH RAINBOW ORCHID

Could be best competition for years

A REVELATION is what this reporter calls the intriguing sight of Mr. Julius Chancer accompanying star of the Hollywood silver screen – Lily Lawrence – to the Daily News offices, for it does nothing but confirm the fact that the camp of Lord Lawrence is uniting with that of Sir Alfred Catesby-Grey to enter the mysterious rainbow orchid – the effect being none other than a botanical war with the black pearl

This has gone far enough, Jules. I refuse to play Pickle's game and, as far as I'm concerned, the rainbow orchid matter is at an end!

You can't mean that, Sir Alfred!

Apart from the money we need, it will get us out of this...of this...antique-finding service we've become!

We do *not* deal in antiques! Our work is far more important than that, as you well know.

If you decide to follow this then you will be entirely on your own!

Elsewhere...

TOK TOK

Come in, Pendleby!

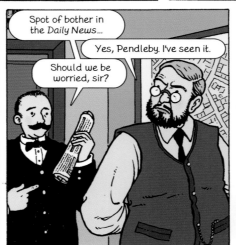

Spot of bother in the *Daily News*...

Yes, Pendleby. I've seen it.

Should we be worried, sir?

No, not yet. Let's keep a close eye on developments though, shall we? Get Mr Drubbin out in the field.

At once, sir.

And...

Oh, dear.

Oh, dear me.

Oh, deary, deary me.

Also...

Is Pickle still ignoring us, Evelyn? Despite Box's little arm-twisting?

I'm afraid it's a bit more serious than that, Mr Grope.

So, Lawrence is involved with this rainbow orchid, is he? Too bad. We'll have to put a stop to that...oh, yes... a very definite stop to that!

Two days later...

Julius!

Thank heavens you're here at last!

What's wrong, Lily?

It's my father. He's lost his mind!

What do you mean?

He's locked us all out of the house. He's been drinking.

It's all right. He can't stay in there forever.

He's not in the house, he's on it. Look!

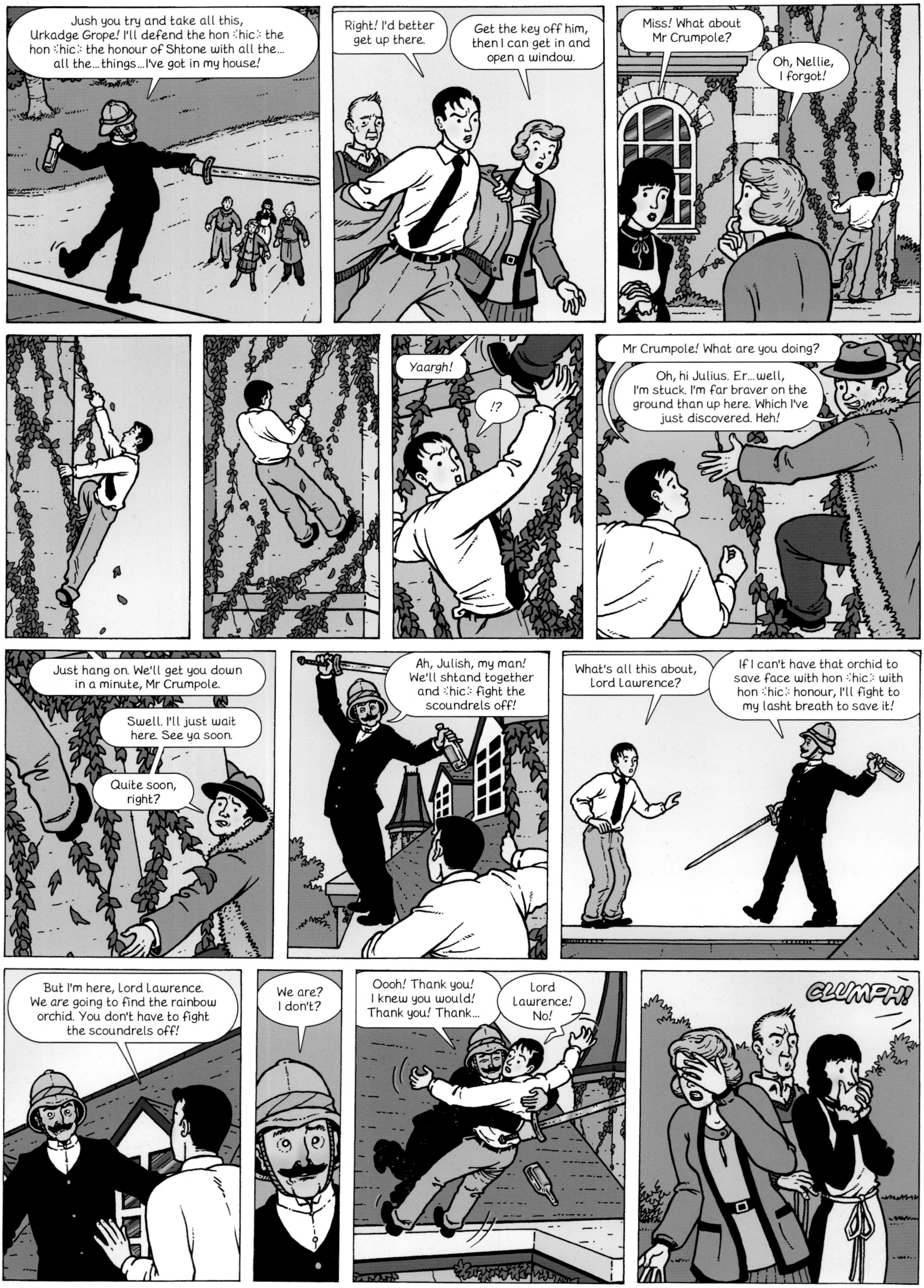
Jush you try and take all this, Urkadge Grope! I'll defend the hon *hic* the hon *hic* the honour of Shtone with all the... all the... things... I've got in my house!
Right! I'd better get up there.
Get the key off him, then I can get in and open a window.
Miss! What about Mr Crumpole?
Oh, Nellie, I forgot!
Yaargh!
!?
Mr Crumpole! What are you doing?
Oh, hi Julius. Er... well, I'm stuck. I'm far braver on the ground than up here. Which I've just discovered. Heh!
Just hang on. We'll get you down in a minute, Mr Crumpole.
Swell. I'll just wait here. See ya soon.
Quite soon, right?
Ah, Julish, my man! We'll shtand together and *hic* fight the scoundrels off!
What's all this about, Lord Lawrence?
If I can't have that orchid to save face with hon *hic* with hon *hic* honour, I'll fight to my lasht breath to save it!
But I'm here, Lord Lawrence. We are going to find the rainbow orchid. You don't have to fight the scoundrels off!
We are? I don't?
Oooh! Thank you! I knew you would! Thank you! Thank...
Lord Lawrence! No!
CLUMPH!

Thank... you... *hic!*

HOOOOOOO-JEEE!

THUNK!

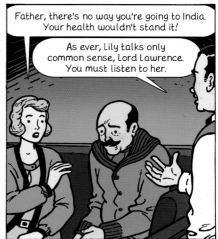

Much...better... down here...

Ow.

A bit later...

Julius, I don't know what happened to me. I can't apologise enough...

Let's forget it, Lord Lawrence. The important thing now is to get this expedition going as soon as possible.

I think I just need a couple of days, maybe a week.

Father, there's no way you're going to India. Your health wouldn't stand it!

As ever, Lily talks only common sense, Lord Lawrence. You must listen to her.

I'll have you know I was at Ladysmith!

Yes, father, almost thirty years ago!

See what she's saying, Lord Lawrence? Pure logic.

No. My mind is made up. I will go in your place.

What!? You can't! In three months we start shooting *Melody of Life.* It's too dangerous! Think of your fans!

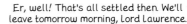
She's gone totally screwy! She's spouting horsefeathers! Sir, say something! You were at Ladysmith!

The Wembley Exhibition is in six weeks, Nathaniel. We have to be back by then anyway.

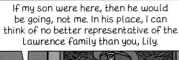

If my son were here, then he would be going, not me. In his place, I can think of no better representative of the Lawrence family than you, Lily.

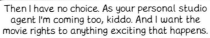

Then I have no choice. As your personal studio agent I'm coming too, kiddo. And I want the movie rights to anything exciting that happens.

You will go back to United Players, Nathaniel. This has nothing to do with Hollywood. Sorry.

Er, well! That's all settled then. We'll leave tomorrow morning, Lord Lawrence.

Tomorrow? Yes, yes of course. Thank you, Julius.

later the same day...

Sir A —
Even if we don't find the orchid we do need the funds!
I can understand your view, but don't agree with it. and still wish you'd come along.
I am going to the Stone Estate and plan to start as soon as possible.
— At least — even now — give me your blessing.
Your loyal assistant —
Jules

Ah, Charlotte...

Sir Alfred! You're not going to let him go on his own are you?

Julius has made his decision.

Well, I can have you packed in no time, and you can join him before lunch. In fact you can take lunch with you. Now, let's see, I've got plenty of bread, some cheese...What fruit?

Charlotte, this whole scheme has been baked out of *nothing!* The story didn't even exist until that reporter, Pickle, created it! I *refuse* to play along with such a sensation, my research must come first.
As for Lord Lawrence, he drank his problems from a whisky bottle, and I have little sympathy with that!

A little more sympathy for Julius might not go amiss, Sir Alfred, if I may say so!

Julius is more than capable. He'll be capable in India just as he was in the Lost Tunnels of Achi Baba.

Now, he asked for my blessing, and I'm going to send it to him. I'll be back within the hour.

Sir Alfred! What a coincidence!

Ah, Mr Pickle. Yes, I'm sure it is.

Well, as you're here, just one important question...

Can you give my readers some information on the rainbow orchid you plan to enter at Wembley?

Great!

Certainly.

Orchis ouranio-toxo is caenogenetic and genus *Apostasioideae*, subclass Monocatyledonae. It is zygophotic and hortensial, but not esculent. But is it a *Paphiopedilum* or a *laeliocattleya*? We just don't know!

Er, wait...

Its iridisation is septochromatic. It is an epiphytic herbaceous perennial and relies on mycorrhizal nutrients. But you probably already knew that.

Um...

Good day, Mr Pickle.

Good day...

COLONIAL
MISSIONARY
SOCIETY
Founded 1794

COLONIAL
MISSIONARY
SOCIETY
Founded 1794

Well, well. That's Sir Alfred Catesby-Grey!

ROYAL MAIL
LINE
STEAM PACKET COMPANY
CRUISES DE LUXE BY
R M S P "ARCADIAN"

The next morning...

Nellie, have you seen Mr Crumpole this morning?

Oh, Miss, I thought you knew. A taxicab collected him before breakfast. He was all packed.

Oh.

Your father's supplied us with more than we need, Lily... is everything all right?

It's Nathaniel. He left without saying a word. I feel terrible.

Never mind. He'll be better off back in Hollywood.

Hello, what's this?

Morning, Lord Lawrence.

Thank you.

The post. There's a package and a letter addressed to you, Julius! Just one for me.

They're from Sir Alfred! He says he's found out where Father Joseph Pinkleton retired to...a small village called Hasan Wahan near Mohenjo. Also the name of a contact in Karachi, Major Fraser-Tipping.

Plus a rubbing of the Indus stone tablet!

Oh!

It's from Urkaz Grope! "Remember, The Black Lion devoured his lords."

The Black Lion? What on earth does that mean? Does he mean his orchid?

I...er... I have no idea...I don't know.

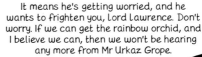

It means he's getting worried, and he wants to frighten you, Lord Lawrence. Don't worry. If we can get the rainbow orchid, and I believe we can, then we won't be hearing any more from Mr Urkaz Grope.

Julius, I hope you're right.

Back in town...

The Daily News

DRRRIIIINNGGG!

DRRRIIIINNGGG!

William Pickle, *Daily News*...What? When?...
Right...Which station?...No...I didn't know...I'm
not in their good books, obviously...*ha ha*, yes...
Thanks for the tip-off, Harry, I owe you!

George! Get your camera!

What's going on?

Not sure. There's a Lily Lawrence
press conference at Main Street Station,
but we have to get our skates on!

DRRRIIIINNGGG!

DRRRIIIINNGGG!

What now?

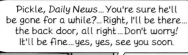

Pickle, *Daily News*...You're sure he'll
be gone for a while?...Right, I'll be there...
the back door, all right...Don't worry!
It'll be fine...yes, yes, see you soon.

Change of plan. Give me the camera.
You're covering the station job on your own.

But *I'm* the
photographer! Where
are you going?

Just get *moving!* And make sure
you get something the others don't!

Meanwhile...

Now, what was the
title of that abysmal article
again, Miss Crow?

*Early Egyptian
Settlers of the Grand
Canyon*. It appeared
in *The Journal of
Historical Exploration*.

Confound having to
remember this tedium!
I should have given Lawrence
more of my home-made with
the special ingredient, then
I wouldn't have to do this.

Here we
are, Scobie.
Pull up.

Sir Alfred, there's a gentleman asking to see you, a Mr Grope.

Urkaz Grope? Hmm. All right, I'll see him.

Can't this orchid affair leave me in peace?

Sir Alfred Catesby-Grey! What a tremendous honour to meet you at last!

Mr Grope. I'm sorry, but I only know your name from recent articles in the press, in which my own name also unwillingly appears.

Then we are united in that unwillingness! These people can only jealously criticise those of us who actually do something *worthwhile* in this world.

Quite so, Mr Grope. And what is it that you do in this world?

Oh, business is my business! Overseas and at home. I have ten fingers, Sir Alfred, each one in its very own pie. But what about you? How I marvelled at *Early Egyptian Settlers of the Grand Canyon* in *The Journal of Historical Exploration*. Such expertise!

And now a botanist too, I understand?

Just a hobby. Even so, I've never heard of a black pearl orchid before.

And I'm assured by my experts that there is no such flower as a rainbow orchid. It's an interesting situation, wouldn't you agree?

Mr Grope, I have no interest in the Wembley competition. Lord Lawrence has merely hired my assistant for an expedition to search for an orchid that may or may not exist.

You mean...you don't actually *have* the orchid?

Lawrence is even more desperate than I thought! Well, well, *heh!* And all over a silly little sword I took a fancy to.

I understand ownership of that sword goes hand in hand with the Stone estate.

Oh, I'm sad to say Lawrence is a terrible fabulist! He probably told you that absurd story about the Crusade, and his father at Kandahar.

What spoofery!

Well, Sir Alfred, I must let you return to your study of...of all this, er, *old stuff.* I adore old stuff myself! And please, don't worry about this orchid business. Just a silly wager between two old fuddies!

So I see, Mr Grope.

Miss Crow, make sure this Lawrence expedition does not return with their orchid, or any other flower. Perhaps they shouldn't even return at all.

The Trembling Sword of Tybalt Stone must be mine!

They won't even sniff a buttercup, Mr Grope.

At that moment, elsewhere...

Wow! Grope lives like a king!

But it's the back door for the likes of me!

TOK! TOK!

TOK! TOK!

We haven't got long. Mr Grope could be back soon!

Once I've done this, Mr Pickle, we're even. You can't ask me for anything else.

Maybe. Just don't forget who exposed your creditors in *The Daily News* and saved you from being thrown into a canal wearing cement-filled boots.

I'd never have thought working with tulips could be so dangerous. And bringing you here, I'm starting to feel less secure about orchids too.

Well, here she is...

Teeth of a ghost! What a flower...it's stunning! It really is black...bottomless!

Beautiful, isn't she?

Er...sorry, what are you doing, Mr Pickle?

My job, Newton. My readers will want to see a picture of this famous black orchid.

No, no, no! You can't! If Mr Grope finds out you've been here...

Oh, you'll be fine. Now get out of the way!

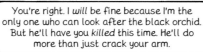

You're right. I *will* be fine because I'm the only one who can look after the black orchid. But he'll have you *killed* this time. He'll do more than just crack your arm.

Oh you're blithering, Newton.

Now, move!

No! You have no idea what Grope is planning!

BOK!

YAARRGH!

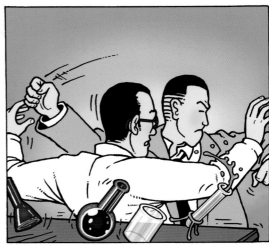

Ak!

Nnnng!

CHK!

Sorry! Sorry, Mr Pickle! Stop. Let's talk about this...

Well...all right. You'd better tell me something good.

If Urkaz Grope wins the orchid competition, he's giving me all the prize money. If you promise not to print a word more of all this, I'll...I'll give you half.

I don't understand. Why enter the competition if he doesn't want the money?

If I told you that, our lives wouldn't be worth a shilling of it. This is big, and Mr Grope is a dangerous man with people in every corner of the world.

You've got me wrong, Newton. I'm not interested in money. I just want to give my readers a good story. The scoop. I'll find out what Grope is up to without your help.

Uh-oh!

I have a good story for you, Mr Pickle. It's about a reporter who disappeared from the face of the Earth, never to be seen again.

Yes, it has a certain something, don't you think?

Back in town...

MAIN STREET

We'll avoid the passenger lines and from Southampton get a boat to Cherbourg. The fastest mail vessels leave there for Port Said, with just one stop at Gibraltar.

From there, we'll see what can get us down the Suez and on to Karachi with the minimum of fuss.

That sounds good to me and, most importantly, helps us to keep a low profile!

Lily!

Do you think sound pictures are going to catch on? Would you make one?

Will your next film be a comedy?

Have you been recalled by the studio?

Lily!

Will Lubitsch direct you?

How did they know...?

Gentlemen...

Thank you for coming to this Lily Lawrence press gathering, where United Players have a very special announcement to make!

Nathaniel!

But first we just need to finalise a last-minute detail! Back in a moment.

Charles, keep them occupied.

Erm, well, yes... now, I expect you have all wondered, at some point, er, how does a moving picture star, like, you know, Miss Lawrence, get to her important functions, indeed, like this one, on time? Well, that is the job of the chauffeur...

Nathaniel, what are you doing here? What are the press doing here?

I got thinking. You said your trip had nothing to do with Hollywood, but you're as wrong as a blue rat playing the trumpet!

I'm your publicity agent and this expedition is big news. So that's big news for United Players. Furthermore, it is my job, by contract no less, to look after you and make sure you're at the studio to shoot your next movie. So, I'm sticking with you, kiddo!

We'll have to discuss all that later, but right now we have to get rid of the press. We can't publicise this trip, Mr Crumpole. It may even be dangerous to do so.

Dangerous?

Now, I have an idea. Here's what we'll do...

...and so that's how, adding just a touch of vinegar and some lemonade, I can get such a good shine to come up on the motor car.

Right. This is your exclusive, and I won't be taking questions. Lily, with myself and her scriptwriter here, is leaving for France to work on a new story for a movie to be filmed at Elstree. Ivor Novello will co-star.

Who'll direct? Hepworth?

What's the picture called?

Isn't Novello contracted to Adrian Brunel?

Is Lily moving to British International?

That's all there is!

Now... SKADOODLE!

Handled nicely, Mr Crumpole.

Call me Nat!

Um, excuse me. I didn't know you were a scriptwriter, Mr Chancer. Don't you work for Sir Alfred Catesby-Grey?

Ah, George Scrubbs, how nice to see you. Well, as we have, um, a special relationship with *The Daily News*, I suppose it won't do any harm to give you the truth.

Wow! I'd really appreciate that!

I'm just the historical advisor. It's a period film, you see.

I see!

Yes, we're meeting the writer in France. I can't tell you who it is.

Oh.

Noel Coward.

Coward!

You didn't hear that from me.

Of course.

Wait until Pickle hears what I've got!

It's me, Box. They're getting the Southampton train. What's the boss say? Right, I'll see you there. Yeah...yeah. Oh, they'll get on the boat all right, but they won't be on it when it reaches France!

It's a shame the *Aquitania* goes on to New York after Cherbourg. I could quite happily travel like this all the way to Karachi!

I'd feel safer on a merchant vessel. Bad timing none were scheduled.

Still, your hat seems to be doing its job. No one's recognised you so far!

You don't *really* think we're in any danger hunting orchids, do you?

No, I'm sure not. I gave Nat that idea to get rid of the press.

But there was that rather sinister coded threat Grope sent your father.

Yes, that was quite odd. And I hear William Pickle spent a morning in hospital after publishing Grope's name in his news column.

Anyway, let's find Nathaniel and join him for that cup of tea he went in search of!

At least we've left Urkaz Grope, the press and all those complications behind us. Just plain sailing from here on!

You're what?

I feel...very ill indeed...I've never been on a ship before... I didn't know I'd...oooohh!

You can survive ten rounds with Jack Dempsey but you can't stand up on a boat. Wonderful.

So much for your grand plan to heave our friends overboard halfway across the channel!

Wuughh... don't use that word!

What, heave? Heave? Don't say heave? Why not say heave?

Yaauughh!

A rethink is in order. Now, we do have the banana operation. If we can...

Wait!

Is that...? Yes, it's Crumpole! Lily's agent!

And he's on his own!

I just need a few little bits. Things could be looking bright again!

Uurrrgh... stop the cabin moving!

Crumpole? Mr Nathaniel Crumpole? The famous Hollywood agent?

Well...er, yes. Yes, that's me.

I knew it! I never thought I'd get this close to such an influential and well respected talent in the world of moving pictures!

Oh, ha ha! Really?

I'm Evie! I'm an actress! I'd love to be in one of your pictures, Mr Crumpole, you make the best!

Oh, I don't really make movies... not yet, anyway. But I expect United Players to move me into writing or directing very soon. I give them lots of ideas, you see.

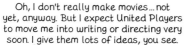

Ooh, I bet you're full of big ideas! I bet you even have a script in your head right now, or...I know! You're on one of those research trips I read about in *Picture Show*!

How exciting! Even a tiny part in a Crumpole picture would be a dream! What's it about?

Ah, we movie makers have to keep such trips top secret, I'm afraid. Just a little adventure set in India. You're obviously a talented girl, contact me when I get back from Karachi and we'll make you a star.

Thank you, Mr Crumpole! I won't tell a soul, I promise!

Lily, do you recognise that girl?

Oh! It can't be!

Ah, there you two are! Er... what's wrong?

Do you know who that *friendly* young lady was, Nat?

Sure do, her name's Evie.

Hey, she only recognised me because she's an actress and she loves my work. I can't fool my fans. I didn't mention you, Lily!

You didn't have to. That was Evelyn Crow, Urkaz Grope's personal assistant. She must be following us.

No, she said... she said... *really?* But why would she follow us?

Grope must know we're after the orchid for Lord Lawrence. So what else does 'Evie' know?

Well, Nathaniel?

Hojee! I... I might have mentioned India, I think, just a little bit.

Not good, but India's a big place.

Ah... um, if I mentioned, say, Karachi, would that also be not good?

In an hour the *Aquitania* leaves for New York. Nat... I'm wondering if it might be best if you booked a cabin.

No! I have to look after Lily! It's my job! I couldn't help... messing... up.

I'm really sorry, Nat, but doing your job just seems to attract trouble.

Look, for now you two stay here while I go and find a mail ship that can get us to Port Said. I won't be long.

Lily, what can I do? I promise not to attract any more trouble. I won't have any more bright ideas... I'll stick by your side through thick and thin... I'll...

...I'll...

I don't know, Nathaniel...

...Maybe this just isn't your sort of thing. Maybe you'd be better off doing what you do so well back at United Players...

Maybe...

Nathaniel...?

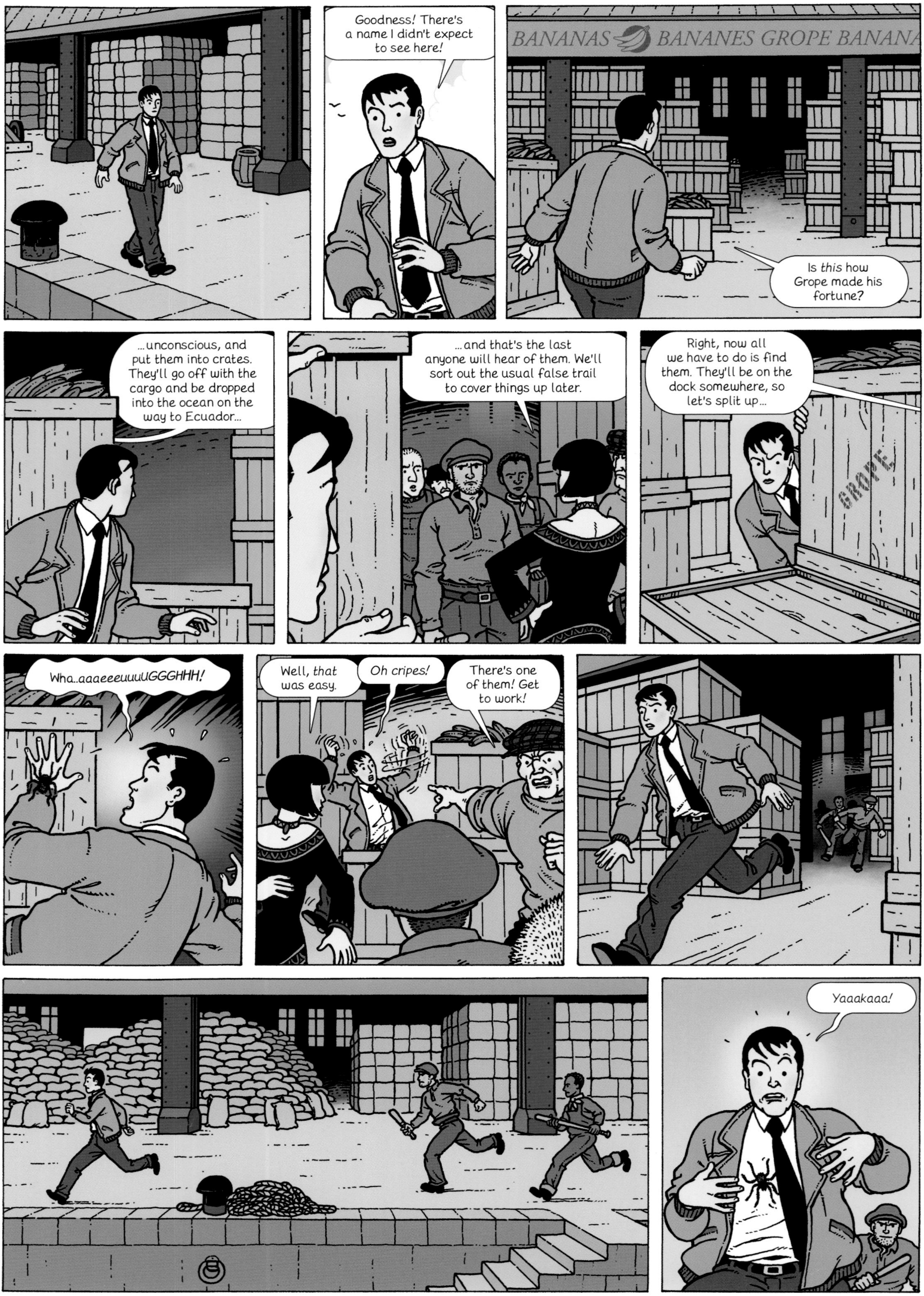
Goodness! There's a name I didn't expect to see here!
BANANAS BANANES GROPE BANANA
Is *this* how Grope made his fortune?
...unconscious, and put them into crates. They'll go off with the cargo and be dropped into the ocean on the way to Ecuador...
...and that's the last anyone will hear of them. We'll sort out the usual false trail to cover things up later.
Right, now all we have to do is find them. They'll be on the dock somewhere, so let's split up...
GROPE
Wha..aaaeeeuuuUGGGHHH!
Well, *that* was easy.
Oh cripes!
There's one of them! Get to work!
Yaaakaaa!

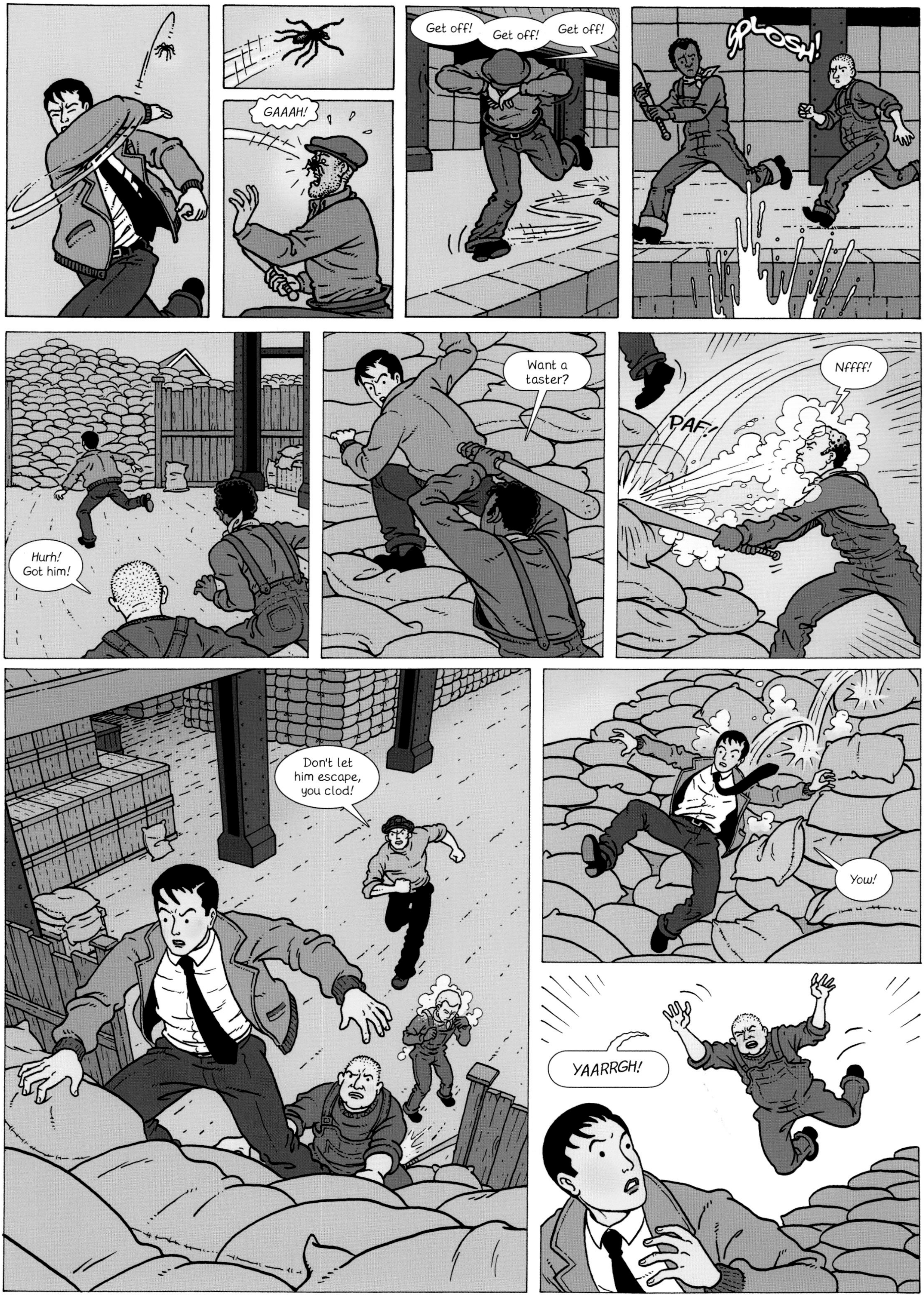
GAAAH!
Get off!
Get off!
Get off!
SPLOSH!
Hurh! Got him!
Want a taster?
PAF!
Nffff!
Don't let him escape, you clod!
You!
YAARRGH!

kof!

No!

WAK.

Did I get him?

Idiot.

Lily! I ran into...

Where's Nat?

I don't know, he just went off! You *both* just went off!

We have to get away. Grope's got a warehouse here, and Evelyn Crow has henchmen out for us.

Gracious. Urkaz Grope really does want to win that competition, doesn't he?

Hey!

I've found something you two are going to love!

Nat... where did you... what... Oh, it doesn't matter! We must get away from here. Now!

Lily, don't you recognise that name? No? I didn't at first. What about these movies... *Wings, Sky Devils, Hearts of Brass?*

Tayaut...? Not Benoît Tayaut? The Hollywood stunt pilot? But, we know him!

That's his daughter, Josette, pasting up posters! His aerodrome is a mile away! We could save two weeks of sailing...

...he could fly us to Karachi!

Hey! There's that actress, Evie!

They're over here! QUICK!

Who's she shouting to? What's going on?

If we don't move it, we're likely to be boxed up in banana crates and shipped to Ecuador!

Oh. Well, Josette has transport. She said she'd wait by the West Gate!

Is there a choice?

All right...

Leave the suitcases, just bring the packs!

On the double! Don't let them get away this time!

Almost there! There she is!

That? That's the transport?

Josette! We appear to have a pack of mobsters after us!

Vite! Jump on!

On board!

On y va!

They're going to catch us up, this thing moves at a crawl!

What are we going to do? They're laughing at us!

Bring 'em on! Except maybe that one at the back. He's a bit big!

Wait, I've got a surprise for them.

Let them come up close!

Hey! Pull over! I want to give you a speeding ticket!

Hurh hurh hurh!

Now!

SPAK!

Hey, Julius! We're giving them a good pasting! Ha ha!

SPAK!

Wooaah!

Nathaniel!

Hello, movie man.

What *me*? No no, you're after that other movie guy!

Turn the engine off, girl!

Or shall we stop it by getting rid of the driver?

YAAAGGHHH! Hot! Hot!

TTSSSSSSSSSS

Sure, he looks like me, but he wears a hat. Look, no hat here!

You'll do. Your friends will come back for you.

You think?

Nat, run! Let's go!

GLOP!

mmmffspmmffglmph!

Gah! He's going to regret doing that!

Back to the warehouse! We'll get reinforcements, just to make sure.

TAYAUT

Chief, Josette is back from the docks. Who's that with her?

It looks like...but it cannot be! Is that Lily Lawrence?

Benoît Tayaut!

Monsieur Crumpole! What on earth are you doing here? I'm delighted! I haven't seen you since *Hearts of Brass!* Have you come to see my show?

Monsieur Tayaut, I'm afraid we're in a spot of bother, and, well...

We're interested in hiring your services!

Ah! Let us go to my office, mes amis, and we'll discuss! Please...

Fifteen minutes later...

Yes, we've had trouble from the banana warehouse ourselves. They tried a protection racket on us.

And failed!

So, what are your thoughts on a flight to Karachi, Monsieur Tayaut? Can it be done?

Yes, the Breguet could do it. Including refuelling at Amman...I would say it would take about forty hours.

When would we leave?

At your convenience, Benoît. My father would contribute a sizeable sum to the *Cirque d'Avion*.

A generous offer, which I accept! Josette, get your sister and pack my long-haul bag and charts.

Oui, Papa!

There is no time like the present, and besides, the weather now is good, tomorrow is uncertain. So...allons-y!

And so...

Josette, thanks for your help getting us away from the dock.

I am Eloise. Josette is over there. We are twins. *De rien tout de même.*

Girls!

The weekend show will still go ahead. Josette, you fly the Fokker for Henri's wing-walk. Eloise, can you lead the aerial clowns?

Oui, Papa.

But, Papa, you need a co-pilot!

I am going to give my new friend, Julius Chancer, some on-the-job training.

Me? But I've never even been in a plane before!

Perfect!

Chief! A truck! Grope Bananas!

Ansel, gather every pilot, engineer and clown! Escort those fruitmongers off our land. No need to be polite!

I'll deal with it, chief! Get going!

Clear the field for take-off!

Step on it! They mustn't get into the air!

BUH! BUH! BRRRRRRRRR

We're gaining!

Not again! Evelyn's going to scream my head off!

Er...looks like we've got trouble, boss!

THUD!

We're outnumbered!

Driver!

...GET US OUT OF HERE!

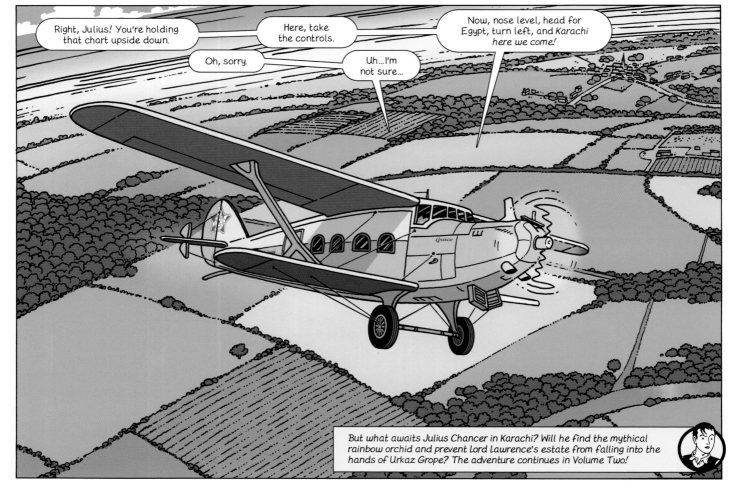

Right, Julius! You're holding that chart upside down.

Oh, sorry.

Here, take the controls.

Uh...I'm not sure...

Now, nose level, head for Egypt, turn left, and Karachi here we come!

But what awaits Julius Chancer in Karachi? Will he find the mythical rainbow orchid and prevent Lord Lawrence's estate from falling into the hands of Urkaz Grope? The adventure continues in Volume Two!

EMBЯ TAYAUT

МЕЖДУНАРОДНЫЙ
СПЕКТАКЛЬ

ПИЛОТАЖНЫЕ
ЧУДЕСА

УДИВИТЕЛЬНАЯ
ПЛНИЗКАЯ ЛЕТЯЩАЯ ПЕ...

Hebdomadaire!
*Cirque Fantasti
d'Avion de* Mor...

TAYAU

SPECTACULAIRE!

J TAYAUT

ÉTONNANT!

...ское центральное воздуш...

WEMBLEY PARK
by train or omnibus
to Wembley Hill
from most stations

Adults 1/6d
Children 9d

A Display by the
**ROYAL
CANADIAN
MOUNTED
POLICE**
Daily

Convention for
**AMATEUR
WIRELESS**
Hosted by
'Uncle Rex' Palmer
Prizes given for Best Crystal Set

**Football Game of
International Stars**
Captains Bob Kelly and Alex Jackson
Sponsored by
THE BOY'S OWN PAPER
The World's Best Magazine For Boys

Have a sip from
**THE WORLD'S
BIGGEST
CUP OF TEA**
in the Ceylon Quarter
with Macfarlane Lang Biscuits

The 9th Queen's Royal
Lancers Re-Enact
**THE BATTLE AT
ARGHANDI**
The Guns Abandoned, A V.C. Won!

Walking Tours Daily
10 a.m., and 2 and 4 p.m
Plus *The Pip, Squeak &
Wilfred Children's Show*

THE FIFTH
BRITISH
EMPIRE
EXHIBITION

To Be Opened
By His Majesty
King of Great Britain, Ireland
and the British Dominions

KING GEORGE V

with a
Grand Choral Fanfare
conducted by
Sir Edward Elgar

Daily orchestra conducted by
JAMES PALFREY
with works by Holst, Purcell, Byrd

All Our Wonderous
Empire And
Its People,
Its Endeavours And
Its Achievements

Adventure on the
**GOLD
COAST**
Railway Line

Visit
INDIA
Realistic Villages, Shops,
Temples, and The Palace

Parade of Characters from
**CHARLES
DICKENS**
see and meet Little Dorrit,
Pip, Beadle Bumble,
Uriah Heep and Pecksniff

Enter An
EGYPTIAN TOMB
Curator Herbert Hipple

The 5th
**BOTANICAL
EXHIBITION**
Opened by
LILY LAWRENCE
Star of Stage & Screen
Enter the Orchid Competition

The 3rd
**PALACE OF
ENGINEERING
SHOW**
Opened by Tennis Heroine
KITTY McKANE

JULES CHANCER AND CHAS HODGKINS
ACHI-BABA FIND, GALLIPOLI

IDENTIFICATION CARD

NAME
William Pickle

POSITION
Lead columnist
reporter

No. DN 2101

SIGNATURE OF HOLDER
William Pickle
PRESS

EDITOR

The Daily News

...ree with it, and st...
...me along.
...going to the Sto...
...to start as soon as...
...st – even now – giv...

*Your loyal assista
Jules*

...owner of the large patch of...
The latest thing in Hollywood is...
Lily, currently signed to United Player...
Crumpole, who uses brisk Americ...
'Applesauce' and 'Sap' to convey...
Release gave up more – Lily has...
Josephine to John Gilbert's Napole...
film of the same name (yet to...
Her next moving picture is with...
leading lady.

As for Sir Reginald, he hopes...
the fifth British Empire Exhib...
Middlesex, as he again enter...
competition, to be opened by...
He may have won it last year...
his Odontoglossum Nevadel...

SIR ALFRED CATESBY-GREY — ROTARY PHOTO E C

CUNARD LINE
CROSS-CHANNEL RAT...

	First Class.	Cabin. Secon...
Southampton to Cherbourg	£3 0 0	
Cherbourg to Southampton	£3 0 0	
Southampton to Havre		
Havre to London		
Plymouth to Southampton (via Cherbourg)	£4 10 0	
Plymouth to London (via Havre)		£3 10
Liverpool to Queenstown		
Queenstown to Liverpool	£4 0 0	£2 10
Glasgow to Liverpool (via Belfast)	£4 0 0	£2 10
...iverpool to Glasgow		£2
...outhampton to Queenstown		£4
...erbourg to Queenstown		£4

Return Bookings.

...ssengers booking South...
...ton to Cherbourg and
...rning Cherbourg or Havre
...outhampton taking out a
...rn Ticket will be quoted
...ollowing special rates—

...Class Return ... £5

...and Second Class

Passengers booki...
to Queenstown
taking out a Re...
will be quoted a...
special rates—

First Class Return

Cabin and Second
Class Return

First Class one way
and Cabin...

ὑπὸ τῶν ἀνθρώπων ἔνια δὲ ἀνανεύειν· φησ...
γὰρ αὐτὸν εὐφυῆ καὶ φιλέταιρον καὶ
ἐπιδέξιον· καὶ δ....
οὐκ ἐντετύχ...
Ἐκ τοῦ Ἀλεξ...
φυτεύματα ἐ...
δὴ οὐ μονόχρ...
ᾧ τὰ χρώματα

EDNA PURVIANCE VISITS LILY LAWRENCE ON THE SET OF 'NAPOLEON & JOSEPHINE' A UNITED PLAYERS PRODUCTION

United Players

BANANES GROPE
Guayaquil – Cherbourg – Portsmouth
via the Panama Canal

Port De Cherbourg
Entrepôt 8
Cherbourg, France

Monsieur Flue
under the direction of
Mr Urkaz Grope

Fourth Wembley Botanical Exhibition... ...rd R. P. Lawrence, first pri...
presented by Rudyard Kipling. Mrs Minnie Griffin, second prize.

...lds in "Footlights", Special Art Supplement Inside

REGISTERED AT THE G.P.O. AS A NEWSPAPER

FEBRUARY 19th

Picture Show

Every Monday

2d

Lily Lawrence is
"LITTLE MAY"
A Revelation in
the Art of Photo
Dramatics!

See page 10.
LILY LAWRENCE
Interview
"A Day at
United Players"

United Players
Nathaniel B. Crumpole
Studio Publicity Agent, Film Dept.
512 Chaland Avenue, Hollywood, California

Lily as 'LITTLE MAY'

be attending in vain. Yes, faithful readers,
you read it here first – the orchid
competition is a foregone conclusion,
and all thanks to the entry of the
practically unique black pearl orchid, to
be put forward by 'businessman' Mr
Urkaz Grope.

So what is next for Lily Lawrence? Her
father may not take the prize at Wembley,
but he won't lack for the experience and
will send his famous offspring back to
Hollywood in a few weeks with 'plenty',
where she can indulge in more of her
screen capers for the masses.

THE RAINBOW ORCHID
VOLUME TWO

In Volume Two, Julius Chancer's search for the mythical rainbow orchid takes him from Europe to the Indian subcontinent.

Publishing spring 2010

Explore the world of Julius Chancer online at
WWW.RAINBOWORCHID.CO.UK

Discover how the adventure comes to life from script to sketch to finished page, and learn how you can make your *own* comic!

Watch a film of Garen drawing actual panels in *The Rainbow Orchid!*

Sign up as an Orchid Reader and enjoy exclusive content as a member of the Adventurers' Society.

As a member (which is free!) you can read short story comics from the early days of Lily Lawrence and William Pickle...

Adventurers' Society members get all the latest news and special offers in a dedicated newsletter, as well as the chance to enter members-only competitions to win original artwork and other goodies!

Plus...
- *Learn more about the characters* •
- *Reviews* • *Readers' letters and artwork* •
- *Goodies to download* • *Interviews* •
- *Annotations* • *Author's blog* •
- *Volume Two preview* • *and loads more!* •

EGMONT

www.egmont.co.uk